Billie Esplen

COWBOYS AND LESBIANS

Salamander Street

PLAYS

First published in 2023 by Salamander Street Ltd., a Wordville imprint. (info@salamanderstreetcom).

Cover photography by Ella Pavlides and Lidia Crisafulli.

ISBN: 9781914228902

10 9 8 7 6 5 4 3 2 1

Further copies of this publication can be purchased from
www.salamanderstreet.com

Wordville

For Ellsy

Acknowledgements

To Julia and Georgia, muses extraordinaires. To Eleanor Birdsall-Smith, for all the convincing. To my friends, for making my life at all interesting/funny. To Michael Kingsbury at the White Bear, for the space that made this play possible. To my 'favourite teachers' – I'm sure you know who you are. To my wonderful family, and to Fiachra.

Cowboys and Lesbians was part of Pleasance Theatre's programming selection for Edinburgh Fringe Festival 2023. It played at Pleasance Dome from 2nd-27th August, created by the following cast and crew:

Nina	**Julia Pilkington**
Noa	**Georgia Vyvyan**
Director	**Billie Esplen**
Producer	**Eleanor Birdsall-Smith**
Production Design	**Daniel Crilly**
	Charlotte Von Szczepanski
Original Music by	**Billie Esplen and Theo Pepper**

Cowboys and Lesbians was first performed on 18th January 2022 at the White Bear Theatre in London, under the title *Scholar's Creek*, by the same cast. This production was generously funded by Arts Council England.

This version of the text went to print before the end of rehearsals and may differ slightly from version performed.

ABOUT THE CAST AND CREW

Julia Pilkington | Actor *(Nina)*

Julia is an actor and theatre-maker from London. She graduated from Royal Central School of Speech and Drama in 2021 with a Master's in Acting, where she was a recipient of an Embassy Postgraduate Scholarship. She co-created and performed in *Lights Over Tesco Carpark* by Poltergeist Theatre (New Diorama, North Wall, HOME MCR, Pleasance Edinburgh 2018), which won the Samuel French New Play Award. She has performed in *What They Forgot to Tell Us* by BOLD Company (Bold Elephant), *NED* by Lola Shaw (Theatre Peckham) and co-created the show *Move Fast and Break Things* (Summerhall, Edinburgh Festival 2022). She wrote and performed her first solo show *The Oracle* at Camden People's Theatre and Peckham Fringe 2023.

Georgia Vyvyan | Actor *(Noa)*

Georgia is an actor and theatre-maker based in London and graduating from Rose Bruford College in September 2023. Before training, Georgia did her BA at Cambridge. She performed as an actor and musician in her graduate show, *1972: The Future of Sex*, directed by Alexandra Spencer-Jones. Her other credits include: Desdemona in *Othello*, directed by John Haidar; Penelope in *We're Few and Far Between*, directed by Alexandra Sarmiento; Beatrice in *Much Ado About Nothing*, directed by Richard Beecham; and Handmaiden in *Mary Stuart*, directed by Robert Icke.

Billie Esplen | Writer / Director

Billie is a writer and script editor living in South London. She has worked in television since leaving university in 2019, including on the script team for Sally Wainwright's historical fantasy series *Renegade Nell*. Her debut short film, *Home*, which she also directed, won the Oxford University Film Society fiction prize in 2017, and her short film *Vigo* was one of their selected Spring Shorts in 2019. She has both produced and directed for Tightrope Theatre, including Helena Snider's *Nightfall* (White Bear Theatre, 2021). *Cowboys and Lesbians* was first produced in 2022 under the title *Scholar's Creek* and received 5-star reviews for its sold-out run. It is her first full-length play.

CAST & SCENE NOTES

Scenes marked (A)
Reality. Present day.

Nina	17
Noa	17

Scenes marked (B)
The story. Some nebulous 'period' era in the rural USA.

(Nina plays)	Carter, 20
	Finneas, 26
	(*voice of*) Cathy-Mae, 40s

(Noa plays)	Elda, 19
	Abigail-Rose, 25
	Jedediah, 22

Scenes marked (C)
Somewhere in between A & B.

TEXT NOTES

The start of a new paragraph within dialogue indicates a change of mind or a new train of thought.

A [/] indicates interruption by the start of the following line. Side-by-side dialogue denotes simultaneous speech.

No punctuation at the end of a line denotes an unfinished thought or sentence.

The pace of Nina and Noa's dialogue should move fairly quickly. It often feels like they are finishing each-others' sentences. The dialogue in **B** scenes, on the other hand, is theatrical in rhythm and can be filled with long, melodramatic pauses.

NOTES ON STAGING

Adapting for more performers

Though the play was conceived as a two-hander, performers may also assign the characters in the metastory to additional actors for a different take on the story. For this, they may adjust the stage directions as appropriate. Entrances and exits are particularly flexible in this context.

For example, it is probably important that Nina and Noa are both onstage during all the **C** scenes. An easy way to achieve this might be to have Nina onstage watching Noa and Carter's interaction, and Noa onstage watching Nina and Elda's interaction. There is also no particular reason why Nina and Noa shouldn't watch more of the metastory unfolding in a version where it is being performed by different actors. You may even choose to have them onstage for most of the play.

Specific lines, as they pertain to the entrances and exits, may also be adapted/omitted as desired.

Scene Transitions

We used music and lighting to both mark and fill the transitions between scenes, but you might use movement, soundscapes, anything else or nothing at all.

Costumes

When performing the play with just two actors, we found that the easiest way to manage multiple costumes without long change times was to layer them – for instance, both Nina and Noa wear big winter coats, under which were their Carter and Elda outfits. Elda could then remove a cardigan to become Jed, and Carter could add a shirt to his vest to become Finneas. Denim is also your friend – it's perfect for Elda and Carter's universe, but doesn't look out of place in ours either.

The Kiss

Noa and Nina's kiss in the final scene is completely optional. The same level of intimacy could easily be communicated in other ways – for instance, a long, held glance, or their hands touching when passing the tea. However, if you are including it in the staging, please make sure the actors' boundaries are discussed and respected throughout the performance and rehearsal process.

IMAGES FROM THE PLAY'S FIRST PERFORMANCE

(White Bear Theatre, 2022)

Photography: Lidia Crisafulli

2 (B): Carter and Elda's meet-cute

3 (A): "Just make more!"

6(B): "No man has ever loved me right."

8 (B): Carter punches the wall

10 (B): "I can't have fairies hangin' round my little sis."

15 (C): Nina meets Elda

Billie Esplen

COWBOYS AND LESBIANS

School. Monday morning, before registration.

NOA sits in their usual spot, sipping a keep-cup of tea and waiting for NINA.

Eventually NINA enters.

NOA: It's 8:23!

NINA: I missed the 32. My dad made me take the bins out. Had to wait for the 56.

NOA: We've got reg in five minutes. And my tea's gone cold.

NINA: He just doesn't realise how tight my schedule is.

Contented, habitual silence.

NOA sips her tea.

NOA: My new three-mint is delicious.

She offers it to NINA.

NINA: You know how I feel about herbal.

NOA: It's homemade!

NINA: Well it smells like the inside of a lawnmower.

NOA: I had another sex dream about Mr Eustice last night.

NINA: And?

NOA: We were on a really nice walk.

NINA: Oh.

NOA: I couldn't see him but I knew he was behind me. He was talking to me really quietly and calmly about this new lesson plan he'd come up with for our coursework module next term. And then I just felt his arm come around my waist, and hold me in close. We were still walking but he was just holding me, like that. It was the most vivid thing in the world. I can even remember what colour his jumper was.

NINA: What colour was his jumper?

NOA: Brown.

I guess not really a sex dream to be fair. Better. More of a Love dream.

NINA: Ugh, gross.

NOA: Nins, come on. His wife died.

NINA: No she didn't.

NOA: Yes, she did.

NINA: He's never had a wife.

NOA: Yes, but you know. His whole... widowed vicar thing. There's something going on there. He's lost something.

NINA: Any respect for teacher-pupil boundaries?

NOA: Ugh, Nins.

NINA: The last, desiccated drops of his dignity?

NOA: He needs help.

NINA: Clinically?

NOA: No! Just. Womanly.

NINA: Womanly help.

NOA: Yes!

NINA: With what? His washing?

NOA: No.

NINA: Doesn't separate out his whites?

NOA: Nins!

NINA: Just puts everything on a mixed cycle?

NOA: Well, probably to be fair.

NINA: Mum says you can wash anything at 30.

NOA: He's definitely a mixed cycle guy. He's busy.

NINA: Aren't we all.

They nod. Ain't it the truth?

A few seconds of silence. Then −

NINA: Are we

Boring?

NOA: What? No.

NINA: We just spoke about washing machine cycles.

NOA: Loads of people do that.

NINA: We're seventeen, though.

NOA: Yeah and

We've had a fine innings.

NINA: Have we?

NOA: I'm not bored. Are you bored?

NINA: No! No.

NOA: Loads of things happen to us.

NINA: Yeah? Like...

NOA: Mr King accidentally sent me that naked charity photo from his Google Drive last year, that was pretty intense.

NINA: I don't think teachers count.

NOA: No but his cock was in a sock. How many people can say they've seen the outline of their DT teacher's penis?

NINA: Maybe, lots?

NOA: No. That's a bad example.
What about

Both NINA and NOA wrack their brains.

NINA: My uncle went to prison last year!

NOA: Oh my god he did.

NINA: That was dramatic. I went to visit him and everything.

NOA: Is he still there?

NINA: No, he got out on a technicality. They've just moved to Henley-on-Thames.

They are silent as this sinks in.

NOA: Oh god. Nina! This is a disaster!

NINA: No, I actually think /

NOA: I'm wasting my nubile years on a middle-aged man who was bullied in school!

NINA: We're only 17.

NOA: Oh my god we're already 17. It's all supposed to have happened to us by now!

NINA: What could have possibly happened by now?

NOA: Um, teen pregnancy?

NINA: We've never had sex.

NOA: Heartbreak?

NINA: We've never had sex.

NOA: Having sex.

NINA: No we looked this up remember, the average age to lose your virginity in the UK is 16 or 17.

NOA: And we're 17!

NINA: Yeah but we're not 18.

NOA: I will be! In two months!

NINA: That's plenty of time.

NOA: I can't just – do it?

NINA: Look, we've never subscribed to that whole like lose your virginity for the sake of it thing

NOA: No.

NINA: There are loads of different coming-of-age milestones.

NOA: Yeah!

NINA: Like

They both think for a moment.

NINA: What do teenagers even do in films? Apart from drugs?

NOA: Oh, coming out as gay, that's a classic.

The smallest of silences.

NINA: I feel like the only people who actually Come Out these days are like football players and breakfast TV hosts. And obviously <u>Everyone's Queer</u>, so

NOA: No one's Straight, yeah.

Another silence.

NOA: Neither of our parents have even got divorced.

NINA: This is definitely Hollywood's fault.

NOA: Yeah! No one's teen years are actually like one of those stupid / coming-of-age films

NINA: Stupid teen romances, yeah.

NOA: We are perfectly wholesome young women thank you very much.

NINA: No wistful staring into the middle distance for us!

NOA: No... passing out at parties or

NINA: Drawing disturbing cartoons all over our exercise books

NOA: Or sleeping with each other's boyfriends

NINA: Sleeping with each other's dads!

NOA: Eeeww!

NINA: It's a nest of absolute drama queens over there.
(as if settling on a maxim) Be so sensible they can't write stories about you.

NOA: They just exaggerate it all though, don't they? Like, their version of us is just that Outdoorsy Tomboy Girl.
A big dreamer

NINA: Trapped by small circumstances.

NOA: Literally not a single friend somehow. Obviously no boyfriend.

NINA: Books before boys.

NOA: Spends all her time climbing onto rooftops to watch the sunrise

NINA: And being rude about girls who wear dresses.

NOA: With a scathing wit that only her worldly English teacher appreciates.

NINA: He's definitely secretly gay.

NOA: Mm, Brokeback vibes.

NINA: Well, so it's clear he doesn't fancy her.

NOA: And so she gets to defend him against some homophobic bully, who's like her brutish older brother / or something

NINA: Her brother, yeah!

NOA: The conflict! The tension!

NINA: Love interest?

NOA: A boy. Obviously.

New to town

NINA: Dark and painful past he won't tell anyone about.

NOA: Helping out on her parents' farm for the summer?

NINA: Sexy farmhand! Oldest trick in the book.

NOA: So he can have his top off the whole time.

NINA: And he's got like a surname for a first name. Something like Wilson. Or Miller.

NOA: Carter.

NINA: Carter, lol.

The SCHOOL BELL goes. They scramble offstage to get to reg.

NOA: Tell Eusty Noa says hi!

NINA: I'm obviously not going to do that!

2 (B)

It's early morning on "The Ranch". A ROOSTER CROWS.

NOA, who has become ELDA, enters, holding a book. She takes in the glorious morning, then settles herself down to read.

From offstage, we hear NINA as CATHY-MAE, a firm-handed Southern matriarch. She has a thick but unplaceable accent, and talks – like everyone in this fantasy world – in a deeply inaccurate pastiche of the American pastoral.

C-M: (*off-stage*) Elda? Elda!

Would you care to explain to me why I can still see enough shit for a hog's birthday party in my good front barn?

You'd better get in here, young lady. Your brother's made me madder than a wet hen this morning, and I don't need it from you as well.

Elda!

I have worked my fingers to the bone keeping this family afloat since your father passed. The least you could do is give me a little help round here!

Elda!!

(*exasperated sigh*)

That girl will be the death of me!

Unbeknownst to ELDA, NINA enters, as CARTER. He wears a cowboy hat and, otherwise, as little as possible.

Carter does that thing which all teenage girls imagine happening to them where he just watches her.

CARTER: Hey there.

ELDA: Who the hell are you?

CARTER: Name's Carter. Carter O'Connell.

ELDA: No, I mean. What are you doing here? Besides sneaking around and staring at people?

CARTER: I'm looking for the ranch. Smalltown Ranch?

ELDA: Well, you've found it. Unfortunately for you.

CARTER: You work here too?

ELDA: Born and raised.

CARTER: Oh – my apologies, ma'am.

He doffs his hat.

If I'd have known I was talkin' to a member of the family –

ELDA: It's my mamma you'll want. She's probably in the kitchen shouting at Cody and Tanner. They're the other cowboys. I hope you like ropin' 'n drinkin' because that's about all you'll be getting up to for the next six weeks.

CARTER: I been ropin' steers since I could walk.

ELDA: And drinkin' since you could hold a can?

CARTER looks away, pained.

ELDA: You alright? Don't tell you me you're some kind of prohibitionist.

CARTER: We all pick our own poison, I 'spose.

Now ELDA's interested.

CARTER: Now who's starin'?

ELDA: It's just. You're not quite who I was expecting.

CARTER: Well, you're not quite who I was expecting either.

They share their first meaningful, meet-cute glance.

3 (A)

NINA and NOA are in a bad mood.

NOA: I can't believe that happened again.

NINA: Literally every time.

9

NOA: I think we should actually complain.

NINA: What I can't understand is, it's not like they don't know how many people want the Southern Fried Chicken? / Everyone wants it.

NOA: Everyone wants it!

NINA: That's the whole point. it's like – / make more.

NOA: Just make more!

They are in very serious silence about this.

Their heads turn in unison to watch someone walk past.

NINA: God. Mr Crane is looking / awful.

NOA: Really bad. When did he get that double chin?

NINA: Remember how fresh-faced he was when he joined? Like a little tight-skinned spring lamb.

NOA: Now he looks like

NINA: A witch's tit.

NOA: Agh! Nins!

NINA: Sorry. Was that gross?

NOA: So gross I loved it.

NINA: Do you know what's weird?

NOA: What.

NINA We have literally watched that man pass his prime. We knew him with the light of youth still in his eyes. His hopes and dreams still intact. And we've actually watched them drain away.

NOA: Oh god that's / so depressing

NINA: So humiliating.

NOA: He is a freak though isn't he?

NINA: Do you remember when he said that thing about electromagnetism being like sex? And then went

NINA:	**NOA:**
'Trust me, you'll find out when you're older.'	'Trust me, you'll find out when you're older.'

NOA: Yeah that was fucking strange.

NINA: Idiotic analogy as well.

NOA: And how he always used to stand by Kirsty's desk even when there was no work to check?

NINA:	**NOA:**
I'm so glad I don't do Physics anymore.	I'm so glad I don't have him this year.

A contented, comfortable silences. Maybe NOA sips some tea.

NINA: So. Where are we setting it?

NOA: Well it's on / a farm

NINA: a ranch

NOA: so probably like –

NINA:	**NOA:**
The mid-west??	The deep south?

A moment.

NOA: Where is that exactly?

NINA: It's like. You know.

NOA: Yeah.

NINA:	**NOA:**
Texas.	Tennessee.

NINA:	**NOA:**
Kansas?	Oklahoma?

NOA: So is that the mid-west?

NINA: Yeah? Wait, which is the one where

NINA:	**NOA:**
Everyone's really nice?	Everyone has a gun?

They have no idea.

NINA: Something like that.

NOA: Yeah one of those.

NINA: They all just do that accent.

NOA: Yeah that like /

NINA: Yeah.

NINA clocks the time, gets up to go.

NINA: Right.

Aren't you coming?

NOA: Said I'd meet Eusty for essay feedback.

NINA: That is not a thing.

NOA: Wish me luck!

NINA exits.

NOA morphs into ELDA. Picks up her book again. Begins to read.

Enter NINA as FINNEAS, our 'worldly English teacher'. He is wearing old-fashioned glasses. Some kind of dapper little shirt. Is immediately adorable, somehow noble. These things all suit NINA.

FINN enters quietly, as if trying not to be seen by anyone other than ELDA.

ELDA: Finn! You're here!

They embrace.

FINN: 'Scuse me, young lady. That's Mr Abernathy to you.

ELDA: You know damn well I never called you that even when you were my teacher, Sir. What are you doing here?

FINN: I'm here to convince you to see the light, young lady. What's this I hear about you giving up on going to college?

ELDA: Not all of us can be true scholars like you, Finn.

FINN: 'Oh full of pain this intellectual being. / Our final hope is flat despair.'

ELDA: 'Our final hope is flat despair!'

FINN: Teaching human baseballs like your brother how to spell the words John and Steinbeck can hardly be called scholarship. You, young lady, will be my singular success. My sole salvation. You are going to college.

ELDA: Oh Finn. You know I love books more than anything. But where on earth would I get the money for that, huh?

FINN: That's why I'm here. They've just created a new scholarship for Underserved Young Women Tied Into Unremunerated Agricultural Labour.

ELDA: But my brother, Jedediah, would never let me go. He says he doesn't want any sister of his Getting Above Her Raising.

FINN: Well he doesn't have to know about it, does he?

ELDA: But /

FINN: You'll be out of the state by the time he can say "Budweiser".

It'll be our little secret.

ELDA wrestles with her demons.

ELDA: Ok. Let's do it.

FINN puts a paternal hand on her shoulder.

FINN: You won't regret this, Elda. This is the start of the rest of your life.

They embrace.

ELDA: Thank you for believing in me, Finn. When no one else would.

FINN: Oh, pshaw.

So, what lump of meat have they got you working alongside this year?

ELDA: Oh, Carter. No, I think you'd like him, Finn. He reminds me of you.

FINN: Do you mean he's

ELDA: (*distracted, dreamy*) He's not like other boys. I think he might have feelings.

The sound of a CAR / TRUCK / FARM MACHINERY pulling up nearby.

ELDA: That'll be Jedediah. You better go. But I'll see you...?

FINN: Same time next week.

FINNEAS exits.

5 (A)

NOA is waiting for NINA.

NINA enters.

NINA: I was bored in Maths so I googled some names.

NOA: Hit me.

NINA: (*reading off a list*) Ok, umm... teacher-wise. Byron. Hogan. Porter. Jesse. Ridge. Wade. Finneas –

NOA: Finneas! I like that. Kind of / sexy

NINA: Refined.

NOA: Perfect.

NINA: Misc ranch-hands how about. Cody. Tanner. Oh, Hudson and Judson.

NOA: Omg.

NINA: Yeah?

NOA: There would so be two beefy blonde twins called that, like lurking around the heavy machinery.

NINA: Jedediah's henchmen.

NOA: Exactly.

NINA: Cool. And girls I think you can kind of make anything double-barrelled. Like Emmy-Lou. Fanny-Lou. Patty-Lou. It just needs to have three syllables.

NOA: We could go something stupidly fancy. Like – Esmeralda?

NINA: From The Hunchback of Notre Dame?

NOA: Yeah she's named after that but she hates it and has shortened it to something like / Esme?

NINA: Elda!

NOA: Oh, that's perfect!

NINA: (*as a 50s advert housewife*) Simply perfect!

NOA: (*Elvis*) Thank you, thank you very much.

NINA: (*army toff*) It has been an honour serving with you, Sir.

NOA: (*army wife*) But, Humphry. How do I know if I'm ever to see you again?

NINA: (*army toff*) Don't worry, Phyllis. Whatever happens I swear to you we shall meet again. Some day.

They embrace, then part, wiping away parody tears.

NOA: Well. Great.

NINA: I'll keep researching.

NOA: See you tomorrow.

NINA: 8:05?

NOA: (*army toff*) Yes sir. 8:05 sharp, sir!

NOA exits. NINA sits for a while, basking in the glow of the interaction.

Then she kind of snaps herself out of it...

6 (B)

...and very efficiently and effectively becomes FINNEAS again.

*FINN is kind of nervous. He is smartening up, slicking back his hair –
perhaps whilst looking into that imaginary fourth-wall mirror.*

FINN: Howdy. You must be Carter.

(tries again)

You must be Carter. I've heard quite a bit about you.
Apparently you're not like other bros.

Unbeknownst to him, NOA enters, now as ABIGAIL-ROSE.

FINN: Hey. I'm Finneas. But you can call me –

A-R: Finn?! Finneas Abernathy!?

FINN: Good god. Abigail-Rose.

A-R: Well water my horses, the last time I saw you must ha'
been when /

FINN: What are you doing here?

A-R: I live here, silly. Didn't ya hear? Me and Jed's gettin'
married in September.

FINN: Hold on. You and Jedediah are together?

A-R: Isn't it just wonderful.

FINN: Well, he sure is

A-R: He's a handful, my Jed. But aren't they all. Except you, a course.

FINN: I should say, Abi

A-R: Oh, Finn! Don't use that old nickname on me. You'll have
me all a-flutter.

FINN: I want to apologise for how we left things that night.

A-R: Oh heck, what do you have to apologise for? Leavin' me
on the side of the dance floor like some old milk-less heifer?

Sayin' you were just runnin' to the bathroom but never coming back?

FINN: I wish I could explain –

He touches her arm.

A-R: Oh Finn! Jed could be back any moment.

FINN: No, I / didn't

A-R: But your eyes. Like melted chocolate. I could just drown in those eyes.

FINN: Abi, listen to me. Don't marry that brute. He doesn't deserve you.

A few moments of silence.

A-R: Oh, that's very smart isn't it. Well done, Finn.

'You're too good for him, Abigail-Rose. He doesn't deserve you.'

'Think about what's best for you, Abigail-Rose. You don't have to settle.'

'Oh, Abigail-Rose, you betta watch yourself with that one. He has violent tendencies.'

Anyone can tell me I deserve better. But not one of them has offered to be the better I deserve. No man's ever loved me right. No reason why they would start now.

FINN sags.

FINN: I'm gay.

A-R: 'Scuse me?

FINN: I'm coming out as gay.

A-R: You're going grey?

FINN: (*shouting*) I'm gay, Abi. I'm gay! That's why, all those years ago... It never was to do with you.

A few moments of silence. ABIGAIL-ROSE tries to smile.

A-R: Silly Abi. It's not always to do with you, Abi!

I'm going to go and find Elda. God love her she's being hopeless about these bridesmaids' dresses. Keeps insisting she's going to wear black. To a weddin'! That little hussy could start an argument with a scarecrow.

FINN: I'm getting her out, Abi. It's never too late.

ABI, flustered and confused, goes to exit.

A-R: Well, I'll see ya round, Finny.

FINN: Abi, wait. Please don't, umm, tell anyone?

A-R: You take care now.

FINN takes deep, heavy breaths, as he once again becomes...

7 (A)

...NINA, who is also taking deep, heavy breaths. She is agitated.

NOA skips in, full of good news.

NOA: Guess what.

NINA: What.

NOA: I was rude to Eusty in period five today.

NINA: What did you do.

NOA: He was going on and on about the stupid snake in Paradise Lost being a phallic symbol. And eventually I just said. Sir. Surely not everything can be a phallic symbol.

NINA: And what did he say?

NOA: He said is that a challenge?

NINA genuinely gasps.

NINA: So what did you say!

NOA: I stared him down. Held his eye contact. And then I said. Seriously, Sir. Don't people just get bored of sex? Bored of writing about sex? Bored of talking about sex? It's fucking relentless.

NINA: Did you say fucking!

NOA: No.

NINA: Phew. Then what did he say?

NOA: (*doing an impression*) Noa, people never get bored of talking about sex.

NINA: Oh my god.

NOA: He didn't blink. Just looked me straight in the eyes and said the word sex.

NINA: What the fuck!

NOA: And then he went off on this rant about how there were a thousand different ways to talk about sex without actually talking about sex, and that writers are so interested in it because the only way they can, like, bury as deep into someone's psyche as they want to is by driving that character to the furthest reaches of their capability for violence and cruelty, but also for love and intimacy at the same time.
(*her impression of him*) Sex is what we look like from the depths. Or something like that. That's what he said.

Stunned silence. Then –

NINA: And what did you say?

NOA: That I didn't think that was on the mark scheme.

NINA: God. Maybe we'll never stop talking about sex.

I'm bored of it already.

NOA: Anyway I've thought of the perfect Christmas gift for him. I'm going to make him a card covered in pictures of literary snakes.

NINA: Jesus Christ.

NOA: I found all these great pictures of medieval doom monsters with penis heads in my free period. I'm going to get them done at Snappy Snaps. What do you think?

NINA: I'm sure he'll love having his penises printed on gloss.

NOA: That's what I thought.

How was double Physics?

NINA: Weird actually.

NOA: Oh?

NINA: It was fine. I got the top mark in the class for the practice paper we did.

NOA: That's amazing, Nins.

NINA: But I had this very weird conversation with Susie Webster afterwards.

NOA: What do you mean, what did she say?

NINA: She like – well, she came up to me.

NOA: Yes?

NINA: Which like – already that's quite outlandish.

NOA: Weird.

NINA: Weird. Then she asked me how I was finding Mr Martino's new homework questions. Which I said I obviously thought were / needlessly oblique

NOA: needlessly oblique, yeah

NINA: Which she found funny for some reason. And then she said what are you doing tomorrow evening and invited me to a gig in Bethnal Green.

NOA: A gig?! In Bethnal Green?!

NINA: Bethnal Green, yeah.

NOA: Fuck me.

NINA: I know. So weird.

NOA: That's a date.

NINA: Yeah. Do you think so?

NOA: She was asking you on a date.

NINA: Could just be a friend date, though.

NOA: She's had seven years to make friends with you. She fancies you, Nins.

NINA: She did also say she missed seeing me in Physics when I was off sick last week.

NOA: She's in love with you! She's actually in love with you! God, poor Susie.

NINA: What do you mean?

NOA: Well, it must have been horrible for her when you said no. So embarrassing.

NINA: No I said I would go.

Beat.

NOA: Oh. Yeah, no, of course. So fair.
Like I knew you kind of fancied girls, and obviously
Everyone's Queer, but

NINA: I didn't feel the need to make some huge announcement
when there was nothing actually going on. Bit of a – tree
falling in the forest but never – getting with anyone... type
situation.

NOA: So do you? Like? Fancy her?

NINA: I don't know.
She does have that big mole / right in the crook of her nose.

NOA: That mole, yeah.

NINA: But it would be quite nice to leave school having been
on at least one date. Good to get the old 'first kiss' ticked
off the list, you know. As much as I've enjoyed being a
seventeen-year-old virgin, I think hitting voting age with
my flower still unravished might be a bit much even for my
bulletproof self-esteem.

NINA notices that NOA has gone quiet.

NINA: Is that – gross?

NOA: Gross? No! No, why would it be gross. So fun. Actually so
fun. I'm jealous. At least one of us won't be a freaky sexless
little gremlin.

NINA: I mean we might not even kiss.

NOA: Nice to have someone who wants to, though.

8 (B)

*ELDA and CARTER are working together. ELDA maybe hanging out washing.
CARTER whittling, or something else manly.*

CARTER: So, let me get this straight. The angels really...

ELDA: <u>Share Intimacy</u>. Yeah.

CARTER: Right. But, aren't they all... y'know...

ELDA: Men?

CARTER: Right.

ELDA: They're gay. What's so strange about that?

CARTER: Well, isn't it a bit...

ELDA: Beautiful? It's beautiful, Carter. 'Easier than air with air, if spirits embrace. Total they mix, union of pure with pure desiring. Without love, no happiness.'

CARTER: And they taught you that in school?

ELDA: School? No, they'd've been shocked as all get out if they knew. Finn read it to me. Every Thursday after class. He loves Paradise Lost. Used to say he could never read the final lines without crying.

CARTER: And did he?

ELDA: He made me read them. And then he cried anyway.

CARTER: Would you tell them to me?

ELDA: What? No.

CARTER: C'mon. Give this hillbilly an education.

ELDA: I'll lend you a copy. You can educate yourself.

CARTER: Not sure I'd be much good at that. Never did go to school. My Daddy drunk so much he thought the government were try'n'a brainwash us. Momma died givin' birth to my little sis cos he refused to take her to a hospital.

ELDA: Lord, Carter that's /

CARTER: Is what it is.

ELDA: Your sister. Is she still there? With him?

CARTER: Leavin' her was hard. But I'm savin' up for my own place, then I'm gonna go back and get her. That's why I'm here.

ELDA is hurt by this. CARTER notices.

CARTER: But what about you?

ELDA: What about me?

CARTER: You mean to tell me you plan on sticking around here?

ELDA: What if I am?

CARTER: Working yourself to death for a brother who hates you 'n a Ma who thinks you oughta be more like his half-brained girlfriend?

ELDA: What's that supposed to mean?

CARTER: Well, I /

ELDA: You think I'm weak? You think I don't care about all that? You think I'm a pushover ready to settle for the life they laid out for me, and will never amount to more than a hollowed-out dogsbody shovelling shit and cleaning their dirty dishes at the end of a long day?

CARTER: No, Elda. I think you deserve so much more than that. And I don't believe all the stars in heaven could conspire to stop you from gettin' what you set your mind to. That's how I know you're not planning on sticking around.

A long silence while ELDA meets his gaze, in love with him.

ELDA: There's this scholarship. In the Big City.

CARTER: The Big City!?

ELDA: Shhh! I got in. Finn helped me. And I'm going. Jed's stag do. The night before the wedding. They'll all be so oiled they won't know which way's up. Finn will meet me at the bottom of the road with a bag of my things and drive me as far as the train. And then. That'll be it. I'm never coming back.

CARTER: Phew.

ELDA: So I guess we're both running away, huh?

CARTER: What?

ELDA: I just mean /

CARTER: Is that what you think of me? I'm just some coward ran away from daddy with his tail between his legs when the going got tough?

ELDA: No, I didn't mean /

CARTER: Just leave it.

CARTER paces up and down in his rage. He does something aggressive and self-harming like punch a wall or his own fist.

He's clearly hurt. ELDA takes something bandage-sized and starts wrapping it around his injury. He lets her.

ELDA: Carter, listen to me. I don't think you're a coward. In fact, I think you might be the bravest person I've ever met.

CARTER: You do?

ELDA: I do.

An intense moment is shared. They don't quite kiss.

ELDA Hey, you wanna go watch Hudson and Judson fall into the creek? They've bet each other a lifetime's supply of beer they can jump it.

She exits. CARTER watches her go, in love.

CARTER: Boy, do I.

9 (A)

NOA enters, with her keep-cup of tea. Sits. Waits. She is agitated.

Finally, NINA comes in.

NINA: Morning.

NOA: Hello!

A moment of silence.

NOA: Well?

NINA: What?

NOA: Nins, for fuck's sake. How was the date?

NINA: Oh, it wasn't a date, it wasn't a date.

NOA: Nina.

NINA: It was fine! It was nice. Her brother's band was absolutely awful. So much synth, yuck. He bought us beers though, which like, why does no one talk about how yeasty beer is? He's called Finn actually! How mad. Not like our Finn though. Very, umm, tall with that like Harry Styles hair. He'll probably get famous.

NOA: Right. But what happened? Did you have a nice time with Susie?

NINA: Yeah! I think she thought I wanted to talk quite a lot about Physics, which I didn't mind. But you know. There's only so much to actually say.

NOA: Was it flirty?

NINA: Hard to say.

NOA: Not that hard surely.

NINA: It felt very normal. Just like... normal.

NOA: So you didn't kiss?

NINA: No no no. No.
No.

NOA: What happened when you said goodbye?

NINA: Well, she asked if I wanted to stay at her house because it was a lot nearer

NOA: She asked you back and you didn't go!?

NINA: Well, I had to do my French vocab before bed.

NOA: Nina!!!

NINA: We had quite a long hug.

NOA: Did she – did she go in for a kiss?

NINA: I'm not sure. I pulled away quite fast.

NOA: Nins!

NINA: I don't know!

NOA: So you didn't fancy her then?

NINA: I don't know! It was surreal being that close to someone's face. Are you meant to just...

NOA: Don't ask me!

A silence.

NINA: Do you know what's mad?

NOA: What?

NINA: We know so much stuff. I'd say we're smarter than most adults.

NOA: Definitely.

NINA: Like we're not stupid teenagers. We understand people. How they work.

NOA: Yeah.

NINA: We're basically adults in every single way, except for this one gaping absence of understanding. Like, what if we both just end up sixty-year-old virgins walking through our lives pretending we know what it means to be a person?

NOA: I don't think you have to understand sex to be a person.

NINA: Don't you?
Presumably if I was a person I would have just let Susie kiss me?

NOA: But you don't fancy her.

NINA: No. I don't think I do.

A significant pause. NOA builds up to something.

NOA: The other day, I realised that whenever I try to imagine having sex with a man – just in general, any man – I always imagine it from his perspective. I'm looking down on me. Having sex with me. And he doesn't exist. Isn't that weird?

NINA: Oh. / Well

NOA: So then I thought maybe that's just because we've been conditioned to objectify women? Because all the sex scenes we've ever seen are from a man's perspective. And maybe it's impossible to have your own perspective on it until you've actually done it yourself?

NINA: Yeah?

NOA: So that happens to you too, then? When you imagine having sex?

NINA processes this for a few beats.

NINA: I – I don't think so?

NOA: You can picture a man having sex with you?

NINA: No. I don't think I can picture anyone having sex with me.

NOA: Oh. So you just never imagine having sex?

NINA: Of course I imagine sex.

NOA: But, watching people having sex?

NINA: I'm not <u>watching</u>. I'm not a creepy <u>watcher</u>. I'm just. Both of them and neither of them. It's like a cosmic event and I'm a disembodied entity... hanging out.

NOA: Yikes.

NINA: Wait, so you always imagine you're doing it with a specific person?

NOA: Yeah. I thought that was normal.

NINA: Who do you imagine?

NOA is speechless.

NINA: Sorry. You obviously don't have to answer that. But maybe. If you can't imagine having sex with a man. Have you tried picturing sex with a girl?

NOA considers this. Then, with great awkwardness, does it. NINA watches.

Only at the end of her reverie does NOA meet NINA's gaze.

NOA: Yeah. I think that worked.

NINA: You stayed in your body?

NOA: Yep.

NINA: Who did you imagine?

NOA: Oh. You know. Misc people.

NINA: Misc women? What's that, a quote from a Woody Allen film?

NOA: Shut up. It doesn't matter who.

NINA: Of course not.

NOA: I'm not, like - coming out.

NINA: No.

NOA: Tree falling in a forest and all that.

A silence.

NINA: Oh, so I had this idea!

NOA: Yeah!

NINA: You know in old plays which are called like "The Good Man's Curse", one of the characters always goes (*Arthur Miller accent*) There ain't nothing we can do about this messed up old world. That's just the good man's curse.

NOA: Eeew, yeah. That was actually such a good example.

NINA: Thanks. Anyway don't you think something like that would so happen in our story?

NOA: Absolutely. In like, the most depressing scene.

NINA: Yeah. So what did we say that was going to be?

NOA: Well, we've got the romance plotline down but we still need to figure out where the trauma's going to come from.

NINA: Sex and trauma.

NOA: Sex and trauma.

NINA: Obviously it's going to be something to do with Finneas.

NOA: Him and Jed, yeah.

NINA: And Jed's obviously secretly gay too.

NOA: What?

NINA: Oh, I thought that was /

NOA: He's just homophobic, no? It's not that uncommon.

NINA: I just assumed we were implying something had gone on between the two of them, and that that was why /

NOA: I mean, maybe? It would give him a motive to hurt Finn. But I thought that was the idea with the Abi-Rose stuff. Like. My fiancée fancies you, I'm going to beat you up.

NINA: You're nicer to my fiancée than I am, I'm going to beat you up.

NOA: Exactly. So, Jedediah attacks Finn?

NINA: That's the obvious choice. From a narrative perspective. Drives Elda even further away from her family

NOA: 'How could you? You're no brother of mine!'

NINA: Exactly. And it's kind of her fault, so / like

NOA: So dramatic. So we're killing Finn.

NINA: Aw, it is a shame. What about just like a nice little head injury?

NOA: No. Elda has to be crushed. So that Carter can comfort her.

NINA: But if Finn's dead, she has no reason to stay. She might as well leave, and go and live with Carter and his sister.

NOA: Fuck.

The SCHOOL BELL goes. They both get up to go.

NOA: Let's talk about it at lunch.

NINA: I've got French club. See you after school?

NOA: It's parents evening.

NINA: Oh shit. Well I'll see you there. Get ready to hear Daddy Pete call all my female teachers "Lovely Girls."

They both exit.

10 (B)

JED: (*off-stage*) Carter? Carter O'Connell?

NOA enters as JEDEDIAH.

JED is drunk and struggling to walk in a straight line.

JED: Aren't you going to congratulate me the night before my weddin'?
Come out and face me, you son-of-a-lonesome-whore.

CARTER slowly shows himself.

JED: Oh, there you are. You also been in on this plan of Mr Abernathy's to kidnap my little sis? That's right. I know all about it. If she thought she was going to be carried off into the sunset by some little slicker-than-pig snot weakling like him... then damn. She's more of a half-wit than I thought she was.

CARTER reacts.

JED: Oh, did that hurt your feelings? I mighta known you were a little Mary-Lou.

CARTER: What did you call me?

JED: A little Mary-Louise. A pillow-biter. A shirt-lifter. A shit-shoveller. A dirty little –

CARTER: I'm not gay, Jed.

JED: Let me tell you, homo-sexualising don't hang pretty round here. I can't have fairies hangin' around my little sis. She needs a real man to straighten her out.

CARTER grabs JED by his clothes. Maybe pushes him up against the wall.

CARTER: Don't you dare talk about Elda like that. She is the smartest person I have ever met. And she deserves a hell of a lot better than you are ever going to let her have.

JED: I should have known you two perverts were in it together. Ain't no better friends than goddam good-for-nothing queer cowboys and lesbians!

CARTER: She's gonna get out of here sometime, Jed. Me and Finn, we'll make sure of that.

JED laughs at length.

CARTER: What the hell's so funny?
What have you done to her?

JED: She mighta just found our old friend Mr Abernathy mashed up in a pool of his own blood. Shit, these things happen.

CARTER rushes off-stage.

JED: You better be gone by sun-up, Carter O'Connell. Or my sis might find herself kneeling over another dead body.

JED exits.

It's school parents' evening. NINA waits for NOA in their usual spot.

NOA enters and joins NINA, carrying plastic cups of cheap white wine.

NINA: Oooh.

NOA: I nicked us some from the refreshment table.

NINA: Are they done yet?

NOA: We've got ten minutes at least.

NINA: You were with Eusty for a while.

NOA: Mh... hmm.

NINA: What was he saying?

NOA: Oh, the usual. Tops marks. Good writing. Need to stop stressing so much about workload, blah. What did he say to yours?

NINA: That he was pleased to be my form tutor again this year, and has 'enjoyed my acerbic comments about my peers'. Pete and Janet weren't too thrilled about that.

NINA raises her glass. They clink cups.

NOA: I didn't know if you preferred red or white.

NINA: Oh I'm not / what you call a connoisseur.

NOA: Yeah, I'm not like a connoisseur.

NINA: Oi, oi. Don't mind what's in it as long as it's booze!

NOA: Lads lads lads!

They both make show of 'downing' it. Both silently gag.

NOA: It's all getting a bit tiresome this isn't it? The Dancing Monkey stuff. Thoroughbred Racehorses.

NINA: Firing On All Cylinders.

NOA: We used to fantasise about running away when we felt like this. We don't do that anymore.

NINA: Because we know we'd just get scared. Then homework extensions. It would all still be here waiting. There's no escape for us.

What you want, really – is to be some fur-clad wanderer, huddled in a cave with only a fire for warmth and no one on their way to find you.

NOA: Or like... a cottage. With one really old horse you've had for years and some jars of food and a well of clean water at the bottom of the garden. And, before you get too lonely, an orphaned child who finds their way to your door, starving and dirty, just in time for you to bathe them and swaddle them and nurse them back to health.

NINA: Elizbeth I! Standing at the head of a great hall. Armed to the teeth in satin, hair down your back, roaring over the downturned heads of your courtiers.

NOA: Or a famous opera singer at the turn of the century. Spending your nights under spotlights, then waking up alone in a sun-filled apartment and slipping out of your robe and into a steaming roll-top bath. Alone and barefooted on a really clean floor.

A considered silence. They marinade.

NINA: Sometimes, I'm just desperate to be old already. A writer. Plodding from the kettle to my desk in front of a window full of trees. Sprinkling the preserved remains of my long and eventful life into fiction like pieces of rose-smelling potpourri.

But then other times I'm terrified of aging even one more day. Like what makes me up is the undried sap of my personality, and that the moment I stop oozing, and harden... I'll be a completely different person.

NOA has been quietly tearing up throughout this speech, but by this time is openly weeping.

NINA: Noa?

Oh no. I'm sorry.

We can. Run away. We can.

Let's do it. Let's do it.

NOA shakes her head, still sobbing.

NINA: Noo? What's happened.

NOA: Eusty's

Eusty's

Eusty's leaving.

NINA says nothing.

NOA: Miss Voss told me. He's leaving, Nins. Not even at the end of the year. At the end of this term. So his last day is tomorrow.

NINA: I know.

NOA: You already know?

NINA: Yeah.

NOA: Who told you?

NINA: He did. In reg. Yesterday.

NOA: What the hell. Why didn't you tell me?

NINA: He made me promise not to. I think he knew you'd be upset.

NOA: I am upset.

NINA: And I thought you'd want to me to respect his wishes.

NOA: He's not your dying husband!

A silence.

NINA: It's a nicer school. Out of London. He's buying a cottage. Him and his – husband.

NOA: What.

NINA: He has a husband called Jeremy. It turns out.

NOA: WHEN /

NINA: Yesterday! He only told me yesterday.

NOA: Oh, my god. He's going to think my penis card is homophobic hate-mail!
I can't believe this. I can't believe he didn't tell me that.

NINA: Maybe because he knew you'd /

NOA: Love it so much? I can barely – bear how happy I am. It's perfect for him.

NINA: It'll be alright, Noo. It's only a couple of terms without him. We'll just finish Elda and Carter, go on ignoring everyone and then we'll be gone. Work of a moment.

NOA: I'm going to miss him.

NINA: I know.

NOA: Ugh. I feel like some baby just flailing around hoping to grab hold of someone.
No one loves me.

NINA: Noo.

NOA: Tell me I'm wrong.

NINA says nothing.

NOA: Just Eusty. And now not even him.

NINA doesn't comfort NOA. Instead, she gets up to go.

NINA: I, umm, need to go.

NOA: What? I thought we were going to /

NINA: No I need to go.

NOA: Fine.

NINA: I'll see you, um /

NOA: Bye.

NINA exits.

12 (B)

NOA becomes ELDA. ELDA sinks to the floor, sobbing.

CARTER runs in.

CARTER: Elda, thank god.

ELDA: Oh Carter, it was awful. Finn was so brave. I tried to stop Jed, but I couldn't.

CARTER: What did the doctor say? Is he gonna make it?

ELDA: He's alive, but he's in a coma, Carter. Just lying there, trapped. And this is my fault, if he hadn't been trying to help me /

CARTER: Elda /

ELDA: I'm worthless, Carter.

CARTER: Now you listen to me /

ELDA: Nobody loves me.

CARTER: Don't say that.

ELDA: Apart from him nobody ever has, and / nobody ever will.

CARTER: I love you.

(beat)

I love you.

13 (C)

Slowly, ELDA becomes NOA.

NOA looks around. Not NINA. Instead, still CARTER. They look each other up and down.

CARTER: Well, hi there.

NOA: God, you're fanciable.

CARTER: I think that's kind of the idea.

NOA: Like Matthew McConaughey crossed with / a young Leonardo DiCaprio.

CARTER: a young Leonardo DiCaprio.

NOA: Exactly. Like, rugged, but still pretty enough that / even the queer girls can feel involved

CARTER: even the queer girls can feel involved? I know. But I'm not a boy, really, am I.

NOA: Well, no. You're a manic pixie cowboy.

CARTER: No, I mean. You don't see me as a boy. When you think about me.

NOA: I try not to waste too many thoughts on troglodytes, as a rule.

CARTER: Hey now, come on. I could be the finest male specimen in human history, overflowin' with the full-fat milk

of human kindness, and you'd still think I'd be better off as
well... somebody else.

NOA: No. Yes. Well. Not A Boy is just better than. A Boy.
Obviously.

CARTER: But I'm your fantasy. If you think that then why did
you make me?

NOA: Because. It's a story.

Girls, in stories – we're only valuable if we can convince
people to love us. Right? Well, not "people". You. We get
points for you. Because you make it hard. You get cross.
You're tortured. Your dad runs a cult, or your younger sister
is sick. Your mother is sick. Maybe you're sick?

Your older brother used to hit you. Your dad still hits you.
Maybe you don't have a dad. Maybe you don't have a mum,
then you fell in with the wrong crowd and now you have a
drinking problem or a gambling problem and – definitely
– problems staying faithful. And you always, always have
trouble opening up to people.

Right?

For it to be love, we have to work for it. We have to work for it.

And me and Nins... that isn't any work at all.

CARTER: Well. Then / maybe

NOA: No, that made it sounds simpler than it is. You get to
declare your love. We don't get to do that, not in real life.

CARTER: That just, statistically, cannot be true.

NOA: (*to herself*) Stuff does happen to some people.

CARTER: Why can't you just tell her?

NOA: Every reason. Every single possible reason. And anyway it
doesn't matter because she'd never – she doesn't like feelings.

CARTER: Now you're making her sound like me.

NOA: No. Not in a repressed way. She's content. Intensity rocks the boat, and she doesn't want her boat – rocked. She's happy.

They look at each other for a long time. NOA and CARTER. Or is it – for a brief second – NINA?

But then...

14 (B)

...NOA is ELDA again. She comes back gasping, in the middle of reacting to CARTER's declaration.

ELDA: You love me?

CARTER: I thought you knew.

ELDA: How could I possibly have?

CARTER: Well I do. I love you. But it doesn't really matter because /

ELDA: I love you too.

They don't quite kiss.

CARTER: Your brother's running me out, Elda. Come with me. Tonight. We can still make it to the Big City. I'll take care of you. There's nothing left for you here.

ELDA: I can't leave Finn.

CARTER: He's gone, Elda.

ELDA: No. He's not.

They can't stop me reading to him. Just like he read to me. Every day, come rain or shine, I'll stick by his side like he stuck by mine – when no one else would.

CARTER gets ready to go.

CARTER: Goodbye Elda. I'll never forget you.

He gives a farewell tip of his hat to ELDA, or to the audience, or both.

Then he exits for the last time.

15 (C)

ELDA remains alone on stage.

As she smiles through her bittersweet tears, NINA stumbles in. It is still parents' evening. She has just run away from NOA.

NINA: Why are people always crying near me!

ELDA: Maybe because we're sad?

She looks at NINA properly.

ELDA: Oh. You're sad.

NINA: Why do people always think that? Just because I'm good at emotional regulation doesn't mean I'm sad.

ELDA: No, you are. You've lost something.

NINA: I haven't. Noa has. My friend. She's just found out she's lost her favourite teachers.

ELDA: Like me.

NINA: Yeah, umm... Sorry about that. We just really needed a tragic arc.

ELDA: No, no. It makes sense.

NINA I'm not even sure how Finneas ended up being such a big part of this. It was supposed to be about you and Carter. But there's nothing more important to Noa than a man she thinks is a bit sad. So. Apologies if that kind of took over.

43

ELDA: Wait, am I supposed to be in love with Finneas?

NINA: No, no. I mean you love him, but like, as a platonic mentor. Who also kind of makes you feel romantically validated because he's the only adult in your life who really... respects you. As a full person. Which is maybe why it feels a bit like being in love. Because it's grown-up.

ELDA: Right. So this is the appropriate amount of upset?

NINA: Oh, definitely. It's horrifying. Again, I really am sorry.

ELDA: But I'm in love with Carter?

NINA: Well, in theory, yeah. I mean it kind of feels like you just met, but –

ELDA: We've had a whole summer together. It's been weeks!

NINA: Sorry, sorry.

ELDA: I feel like I've known him my whole life!

NINA: Got it!

ELDA: He's the best person I've ever known. It's the most magical feeling in the world.

NINA: I know.

ELDA: Oh. Really?

NINA: Well, don't act all surprised.

ELDA: I'm not surprised, I'm just pleasantly...

NINA: Surprised. Yeah. You're as bad as my parents. Why does everyone think I'm some sexless little hobgoblin?

ELDA: Well. Who is she?

NINA: Who's what?

ELDA: The girl you're in love with?

NINA: I never said anything about a girl.

ELDA: I know, I'm just goading you.

NINA: Well, I'm not an easy goadee.

ELDA: I know it's not Susie. Not with that mole.

NINA: How do you know everything!

ELDA: I'm nineteen.

NINA: But Noa doesn't even know I'm in love with her!

A shocked silence.

ELDA: I knew it.

NINA: Shut up.

ELDA: Tell her.

NINA: No way.

ELDA: Tell her.

NINA: Why can't she just... tell me first.

ELDA: How is she supposed to know you'll accept her love? You won't even accept her goddam mint tea!

NINA: I don't want to be humiliated.

ELDA: She would never humiliate you. You're the person she admires most in the world. Tell her.

She begins to float offstage, ghost-like.

ELDA: Tell her!

NINA: Where are you going?

ELDA: To the life you wrote for me. Endless menial labour, needless self-sacrifice and one completely sexless romance. Farewell, Nina!

She exits. There is a moment of silence.

NINA: (*guiltily*) Shit.

16 (A)

NINA is waiting for NOA as usual. Nervous, but somehow more at peace.

NOA enters, tea in hand.

NINA: Hi.

NOA: Hi.

NINA: How was the rest of, umm /

NOA: It was ok. Once I'd calmed down. I'm sorry about my Eusty-related outburst. Super embarrassing obviously. I think I'm just

NINA: No, I'm sorry for literally running away. So weird of me. I just thought I wasn't going to be the best person to talk to about

NOA: No, it wasn't fair of me to dump that all on you. And like. Shut up, you know. Shut up about Eusty. I'll be fine.

NINA: So, I actually have something to say. Which it that I do quite fancy you. Obviously.

But I'm not going to be like. 'I fancy you if you don't fancy me we shall never speak again you heartless wench.' You know. I just thought you should know.

But the point is, it will be fine. I'll be fine. I don't have to.

There is long silence, at once weighty and light. Then –

NOA: I obviously fancy you too.

But I think I definitely do have to. If that's ok?

That sounds weird but I don't mean it in a weird way. Sorry if I'm being weird.

NINA: No, I'm being weird. This is quite weird!

They both laugh. NINA puts a hand out for some of her NOA's tea.

NINA: One sip for a special occasion?

NOA: Really!

NINA takes a sip. Grimaces.

NINA: Delicious. Well done.

NOA: Fucking finally.

They kiss.

NINA: We should finish it.

NOA: The tea?

NINA: The story.

NOA: I thought we did? Carter leaves. She stays. They remain young and beautiful in each others' eyes forever. A perfect bittersweet romance. The end.

NINA: I was thinking though – maybe he'd write to her or something? I don't think he would just leave her there.

NOA: No no, you're right. That's actually good. Because then we could have a sequel. Maybe Elda's mum hides the letters from her??

NINA: And when she finds them she decides to go looking for him!

NOA: A road movie!

NINA: And on her way she picks up some kind of comic foil, like a / stray dog

NOA: Lost child! Who refuses to leave her at the end,

NINA: Teaching her the true meaning of unconditional love,

NOA: In a way that no boy ever could.

NINA: And the real treasure was the friendship they made along the way.

NINA: Awww.   **NOA:** Aww!

NINA: Yeah. That's good.

END

COWBOYS AND LESBIANS: DISCUSSION TOPICS

Metastory (noun)
One story embedded within another.
A story about stories themselves.

Parody (this can be a noun and a verb)
A humorously exaggerated imitation of a writer, artist or genre.

The metastory in this play parodies countless coming-of-age films and other stories about teenagers and romance in general. Do the characters in it remind you of any characters in films, TV shows or books? Try to think of a few. What behaviours do they exhibit that recall these characters, or these stories?

Why do you think Nina's character has more affinity with Carter in the play? What traits do they share, if any?

Why might Noa align herself more with Elda's story? What traits do they share, if any?

How serious do you think Noa is being about her crush on Mr Eustice?

Do you think that Scene 8 (B) is the first time Nina and Noa have opened up to each other about sex, and their sexual fantasies? If so, why do you think they feel able to do this now?

We don't know where or when Elda and Carter's story is set. What effect does this have on how we experience it?

Do we know any more about the geography of the USA than Nina and Noa? Do they have any particular factual blind-spots? How might certain political and/or historical truths about the Unites States affect our view of Elda and Carter's story?

What might the future have instore for Nina and Noa? Do you think they get together? If so, will they stay together? What possible reasons might they have for breaking up?

ALSO AVAILABLE FROM SALAMANDER STREET

All Salamander Street plays can be bought in bulk at a discount for performance or study. Contact info@salamanderstreet.com to enquire about performance liscenses.

SHE by Anthony Clark
ISBN: 9781739103057

Seven short plays, for between two and fourteen versatile actors, SHE charts the experiences of different women from childhood to old age. Each with an intriguing twist, the plays are visceral, poignant and laced with humour.

Funny Peculiar by Vici Wreford-Sinnott
ISBN: 9781914228063

In a sequence of four original, cross-cutting, witty and wise monologues four disabled women locked in, shut up and shouted down, give their all to expose the lie of vulnerability.

Trade by Ella Dorman-Gajic
ISBN: 9781914228865

Exploring the currency of female bodies in an underground world, Trade powerfully calls into question the archetype of the 'perfect female victim' by examining the psychology of a morally complex protagonist.

Chatsky and Miser, Miser! by Anthony Burgess
ISBN: 9781914228889

Anthony Burgess expertly tackles the major monuments of French and Russian theatre: *The Miser* by Molière and *Chatsky* by Alexander Griboyedov. Burgess's recently discovered verse and prose plays are published for the first time in this volume.

Placeholder by Catherine Bisset
ISBN: 9781914228919

Profoundly thought-provoking, this solo play about the historical actor-singer of colour known as 'Minette' offers an exploration of the complex racial and social dynamics of what would become the first independent nation in the Caribbean.

Printed in the USA
CPSIA information can be obtained
at www.ICGtesting.com
JSHW012046140824
68134JS00034B/3281